Penguin
and Little Blue

Story by MEGAN McDONALD

Illustrated by KATHERINE TILLOTSON

A Richard Jackson Book
Atheneum Books for Young Readers
New York London Toronto Sydney Singapore

For Mary Ellen, the IRT team, and all the readers of Olathe, Kansas, schools
—M. M.

To Kendra, for her kind heart and infectious enthusiasm
—K. T.

Atheneum Books for Young Readers
An imprint of Simon & Schuster Children's Publishing Division
1230 Avenue of the Americas
New York, New York 10020
Text copyright © 2003 by Megan McDonald
Illustrations copyright © 2003 by Katherine Tillotson
All rights reserved, including the right of reproduction in whole or in part in any form.
Book design by Abelardo Martínez
The text of this book is set in Walbaum Book.
The illustrations are rendered in oil on paper.
Manufactured in China
First Edition
2 4 6 8 10 9 7 5 3 1
Library of Congress Cataloging-in-Publication Data
McDonald, Megan.
Penguin and Little Blue / story by Megan McDonald ; pictures by Katherine Tillotson.–1st ed.
p.   cm.
"A Richard Jackson book."
Summary: Penguin and his pint-size partner Little Blue escape their promotional tour
for Water World and get back to their iceberg home.
ISBN 0-689-84415-8
[1. Penguins–Fiction.] I. Tillotson, Katherine, ill.
PZ7.M1487 Pe 2003
[E]–dc21   2001037320

Penguin missed his friends. All one million three hundred twenty-eight thousand and forty-eight of them.

Once he'd been
emperor, Antarctica's
King of the Ice. Now he
flew solo in a tank with
four walls at Water World,
San Francisco. It just wasn't
the same as diving in dozens,
huddling in hundreds.
He had Little Blue, but she
didn't dive. She belly-flopped,
and two just didn't make
a huddle.

Every day Penguin preened his
feathers, all dressed up for a party.
But there was never a party. He climbed up
onto the highest rock, raised his beak,
and hooted at the sky.

"*Croak! Jabber-jabber! Hoot-hoot!
Nay!*"

Nobody hooted back.

Then one day, after a most handsome dive, Penguin saw
Angela, the Animal Ambassador. She handed them each
a suitcase.

"You lucky clucks are taking your show on the road!
You'll fly to thirty-three exciting places."

"But we can't fly!" said Little Blue.

"Leave that to me," said Angela.

Before they could say "inky
squid," Penguin and Little Blue found
themselves aboard a roaring, silver-winged
bird, sipping Mountain Dews with ice.
      "This big bird flies fast!" Little Blue said.
She tightened her seat belt. Penguin dreamed
of home, where wind sang across cold blue seas,
and glaciers glowed white by the light of the
moon. Temperature: 128.6 degrees *below* zero.
      "Antarctica, here we come!" said Penguin.

When they touched down—no cliffs of white. No sea of blue. Nothing but a flat sea of prairie grass. Temperature: H-O-T, hot!

Kansas!

The Sunset Inn Hotel—a land of potted palms, marble floors slick as ice, and miles of red carpet.

"Home away from
home," said the bellhop.
"Your first show is ten
sharp, tomorrow morning.
Need anything? Press 'zero.'
We want to give you the red-
carpet treatment."
Penguin and Little Blue
looked around the lonely room.
No snow. No ice. Even the ice
bucket was empty.
"I'm hot," said Little Blue.

"There must be ice
somewhere in Kansas."
Penguin opened drawers
and flipped switches.
No ice.

He pulled strings and
turned knobs. Still no ice.

Little Blue pressed a red button.
The room grew hot, hot, hotter.

"Let me!" Penguin pushed a blue button. Cold, cold, colder. "I feel better already!" Penguin said, puffing himself up like the emperor he was.

"Maybe there's ice in here," Little Blue said, opening a door to a room with a tub. She turned a silver knob. Water spouted like a fountain, gushed out of the tub, and overflowed onto the floor, rising inch by inch.

Little Blue looked both ways
down the hall. ICE machine!

They heaped up piles
of ice, hills of ice,
mountains
of ice.

"Wheee!" said Penguin.
"Just like the ice cliffs at home."
"Cool fun!" said Little Blue.
A *knock, knock* came on the door.
"Hotel Security! Turn. Off. The. Water!"
said a voice. "We're swimming
out here."
"We're swimming in here, too!"
called Penguin and Little Blue.

"I'm hungry," said Little Blue. Penguin dialed "zero."

"Room Service."

"We'd like some krill," said Penguin.

"Bagel? How many?"

"Not bagel. Krill. K-R-I-L-L. Any crustacean will do."

"We have shrimp with creole sauce. How many?"

"Nine pounds," said Penguin.

"Dessert?"

"Baked Alaska!" Little Blue shouted into the phone.

In no time Room Service arrived with nine pounds
of shrimp on a silver platter, two cloth napkins,
a real carnation in a vase, and a ring of baked Alaska
browned to perfection.

"Just right!" said Penguin.

"My crop is full," Little Blue groaned, plopping onto the bed.

They played tic-tac-toe on hotel stationery and watched a TV game show. "What's the home of the oldest rock ever found?" asked a face in a suit.

"A: Slippery Rock, PA

B. Bedrock

C: Antarctica

D: Rock and Roll Hall of Fame."

"Antarctica!" shouted Penguin and Little Blue.

"Almost four billion years old!" Penguin told the TV.

Before the million-dollar question came on, the two pooped-out penguins fell fast asleep.

Zzzzz.

At the hotel pool the next morning, Penguin and Little Blue had to sit still and listen to speeches, yak, yak, yak. When their turn came, it was dive, dive, dive. Flop, flop, flop. Afterward, Penguin and Little Blue signed autographs till their flippers hurt.

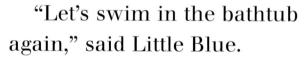

"Let's swim in the bathtub again," said Little Blue.

But before they could say "briny shrimp," they were back on a big bird heading for Boston. Atlantic City. Pittsburgh.

Every day was the same. Dive, dive, dive. Flop, flop, flop. Sign, sign, sign. Las Vegas. Little Rock. New Orleans.

Penguin and Little Blue even tried painting their hotel room black and white, but it just wasn't Antarctica.

"I miss home," said Little Blue.

"I miss my friends," said Penguin.

"You have me," said Little Blue. But two just didn't make a huddle.

Everywhere they went, they had met hundreds of fans. Thousands. Still, not one hooted back.

Then one day, while wandering the Miami waterfront in search of krill, Little Blue stopped in front of a store window. One hundred TV sets! She saw penguins and more penguins, times one hundred!

"Antarctica?" Little Blue pointed. Penguin hooted and brayed and jabbered. But the TV penguins did not hoot back.

"My friends! I've been gone so long, they don't remember me!" moaned Penguin. When he looked up, bobbing there on the waves, was a happy sight: a beautiful sky-blue boat. The S.S. *Admiral Byrd*!

"We've signed our last autograph!" said Penguin.
"We're going home." Penguin and Little Blue put to sea
aboard the four-star cruise liner, and sailed for a week
and a day, to where the Atlantic meets the Pacific.

"Is this the long way to San Francisco?" asked Little Blue.

"It's the shortcut to Paradise Bay," said Penguin.

Gale winds swirled out of the South Pole, music to
their ears. White ice, blue ice, pancake ice, pencil ice,
ice cakes, ice falls, fast ice. Glaciers glistened white in
the pale, blue light, a lantern at the bottom of the world.

Antarctica!

Before their eyes were hundreds of penguins, thousands of penguins, hundreds of thousands of penguins, all dressed for a party!

"Welcome to the Iceberg Hotel!" Penguin said. "All the krill you can eat. Temperature: 128.6 degrees *below* zero. And this is just the tip of the iceberg!"

"Cool fun!" said Little Blue. She put on her earmuffs and snuggled into a scarf. Penguin raised his beak toward the sky and hooted.

"Croak! Jabber-jabber! Hoot-hoot! Nay!" called the others in return.

"There's no place like home," Penguin said, remembering Kansas.

They walked hand in hand to the center of the huddle, where Penguin and Little Blue were warmed by hundreds and thousands of fine-feathered friends.